*S*ocrates is an orphan. His parents have been snatched up by the
dogcatcher, leaving him to live alone in the streets. Abandoned,
hungry, and shunned by the other street dogs, Socrates wonders
if he'll ever have a home of his very own. And, even more
importantly, he wonders if he'll ever find a friend.
Then one day Socrates finds a curious object.
From that moment on, everyone looks at him quite differently.
Whether used as a teaching tool or as a read-aloud treat,
Socrates will warm the hearts of all who read it.

". . . this unusually refreshing picture book boasts one of the most
endearing canines ever seen outside a dog food commercial.
A text that exudes immediacy and originality is perfectly paired with
vigorous artwork both funny and touching."
★ *Publishers Weekly*

". . . this strong picture book can help adults talk to children about
homelessness, loneliness, and acceptance. Its message is for everyone:
we can find true friendship if we put others before ourselves."
—*The Charlotte Observer*

". . . strong, textural illustrations enhance the richness of the story and
provide a glimpse into the world reminiscent of the great French
painters."
—*American Bookseller, "Pick of the Lists"*

"I have never asked anybody to give me their eyes to see. I have always looked at the universe through my own eyes."

    - Muhammed Iqbal

With all my love to Hilde, without whom this book wouldn't be what it is!

    - Gert

For Pascaline Moliter, forgotten little goddaughter.

    - Rascal

© 1992 by L'École des Loisirs, Paris.
English language translation © 1992 by Chronicle Books, San Francisco.
All rights reserved.
Jacket and text design by Alison Berry.
Printed in Hong Kong.

Library of Congress Cataloging-in-Publication Data

Rascal.
    [Socrate. English]
    Socrates / by Rascal and Gert Bogaerts
    32p.   29.8 x 24.5cm.
    Summary: When Socrates, a homeless dog, finds a pair of eyeglasses in the street, the incident
benefits him in more ways than one.
    ISBN 0-8118-1047-X (pb.)
    ISBN 0-8118-0314-7 (hc.)
    [1. Dogs—Fiction. 2. Eyeglasses—Fiction.] I. Bogaerts, Gert. II. Title.
    PZ7.B635783So 1993
    [E]—dc20   92-24120
                                        CIP
                                        AC

Distributed in Canada by Raincoast Books
8680 Cambie Street, Vancouver, B.C. V6P 6M9

10 9 8 7 6 5 4 3

Chronicle Books
275 Fifth Street
San Francisco, California 94103

SOCRATES

story by Rascal

illustrations by Gert Bogaerts

chronicle books

San Francisco

Socrates was an orphan.

His parents had been snatched up by the dog-catcher and
taken to the pound, leaving Socrates to live alone on the streets.
He dreamed of a home other than his cardboard box.
And, more than anything else, Socrates dreamed of having a friend.

He looked to the other street dogs for company, but they just
snarled and growled. They wouldn't share their scraps, and
Socrates was left to rummage through garbage cans on his own.

It seemed to Socrates that he was always alone. Every night, he wandered the streets, wagging his tail at passersby, hoping that one of them would take him home. But the people just looked the other way. "Poor thing," some of them would mutter. But they always kept their eyes on the ground.

Then, one day as Socrates was scouring the street for something to eat, he found the most curious thing.

Sniff-sniff — Socrates examined this new thing.

Sniff-sniff — it certainly wasn't something to eat!

Sniff-sniff — Socrates discovered the thing fit his nose perfectly.

"Perhaps this will help," Socrates thought.

And then he went on his way.

Socrates stepped inside the flower shop. For the first time, no one
chased him away. The florist took a look at him and laughed
a friendly laugh. Then he gave Socrates a quick pat on the head.

Socrates thought the flowers looked brighter than they ever had before.

Next, Socrates went to the toy shop. The shop owner smiled and said,
"Here you go, boy." Then he handed Socrates a bit of his sandwich.

The toys seemed to be smiling, too. Socrates could hardly believe his eyes.

All day, Socrates roamed the streets. Everywhere he went there were smiles, pats on the head and treats. "Extraordinary," thought Socrates as he looked at his reflection. "This thing on my nose must be magical."

As the day ended, Socrates heard music. And when he turned the corner, he found the music-maker. The musician looked at Socrates. "Hey there, friend," he said, giving Socrates a pat.

Then the musician squinted at Socrates and said, "I see you've found my glasses. And a good thing, too. I can't see a thing without them. If you hadn't come along, I'd never have been able to to find my way home." The musician laughed and he stretched his hand out toward Socrates.

Socrates pulled back. "What!?" he thought. "Give back this magical thing?" This thing that had helped him find food. This thing that had made him so many friends.

Then Socrates looked at the musician. He imagined him wandering blindly through the streets looking for his home. He imagined him hungry. Slowly, Socrates stepped forward.

The musician took the glasses. Then he gave Socrates a strong pat.
"Thanks, fella," he whispered. "A good friend like you deserves
a special treat. Let's go home and cook up some dinner."

And then Socrates knew that he had, indeed, found
something magical after all - a friend.

RASCAL committed himself to creating children's books full-time after pursuing several different self-taught careers ranging from advertising to painting. He both wrote and illustrated his first three books, and then decided to write books for other illustrators. He wrote *Socrates* after seeing some of Gert Bogaerts's work. Rascal lives in Belgium with his wife and their two young sons.

GERT BOGAERTS was born in a small village in Belgium in 1965. As a child he enjoyed painting and drawing, and he continued these interests later in life when he moved to Brussels to study graphic arts at the St. Luke's Institute. Mr. Bogaerts now lives in Brussels, Belgium. This is his first book.